Oscar and Arabella

by Neal Layton

Hodder
Children's
Books

A division of Hodder Headline Limited

Oscar was a WOOLLY MAMMOTH.

And so was Arabella.

They liked snacking on leaves and berries,

They liked painting pictures,

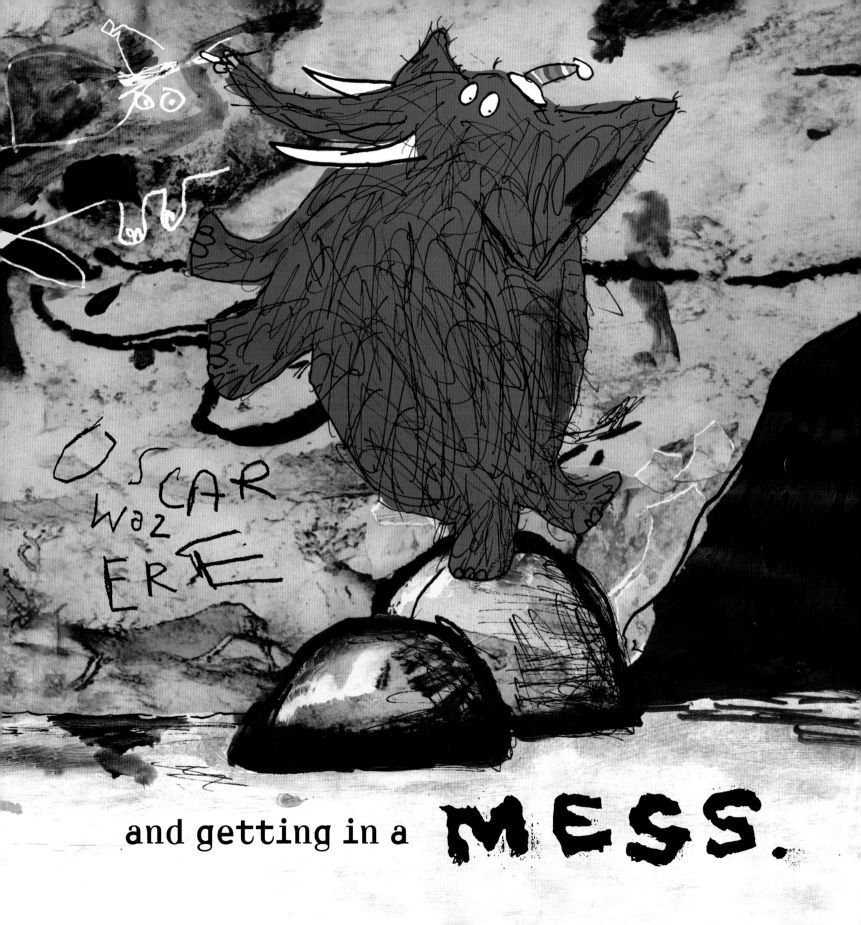

OSCAR waz ERE

and getting in a **MESS.**

They liked
going exploring,

but didn't like the

DARK.

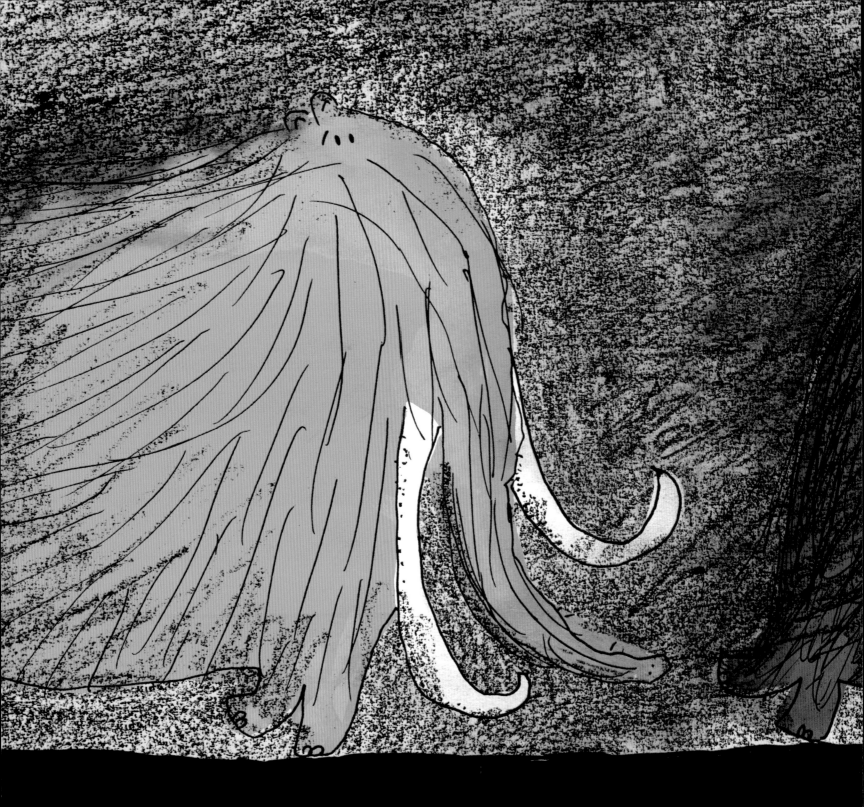

They liked adventures,

as long as they weren't **SCARY** .

They liked making friends,

but not with **wild** and **dangerous** animals.

They liked to keep **FIT** especially when

their lives depended on it.

They liked sliding on the ice,

as long as they didn't FALL OVER.

They liked
climbing trees,

but not too

HIGH.

They liked squirting water out of their trunks, because it was really good  **FUN.**

They liked to go sledging,

but not too **FAST**.

And, at the
end of the day,
they liked
sitting around
the campfire
telling tales
of their
wild adventures
to their
friends,
but not
for too
long...